Thanks for everyth

CW00847268

The FruitHeads admiring the originals:
as drawn by Emiah Jane Elliott (aged 8½)

This Book Belongs to:

....

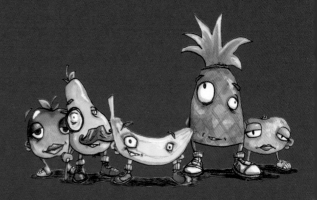

JessPress

Published by JessPress Ltd
Address: PO Box 404, Tunbridge Wells, Kent TN3 0WZ

www.jesspress.co.uk/www.thefruitheads.co.uk

Text Copyright © 2004 David Elliott
Illustrations Copyright © 2004 Edwin Marney
All Rights Reserved

First Edition – 2004

ISBN: 1-905066-00-7

Set in Kristen ITC and Comic Sans MS

Printed in Wales

This book is sold, subject to the condition that it shall not,
by way of trade or otherwise, be lent, re-sold, hired out, or
otherwise circulated without the publisher's prior consent,
in any form of binding or cover other than that in which
it is published and without a similar condition including
this condition being imposed on the subsequent purchaser.

Thanks to:
Chiddingstone CofE Primary School
and
Speldhurst CofE Primary School

The FruitHeads

On the High Seas

Written by: David Elliott
Illustrated by: Edwin Marney

Chapter One

Inside the house, everything was quiet and nothing moved. Everyone was fast asleep, tucked up warmly in their beds.

Outside, night time was fading as the sun began to creep above the horizon. There were no clouds to be seen, and the sky was changing to a beautiful blue. It was going to be a lovely day.

A cock crowed in a nearby field, welcoming the morning. Birds awoke and flew from their nests, looking for the first worm. Rays of sunlight streamed through the windows of the house. It really was going to be a wonderful day.

Slowly, as the sun rose higher, the house began to stir.

The first to awake was Mother. She rose from her bed and went to the bathroom. She washed her hands and face, and brushed her teeth. She then woke her husband and he did the same. Last of all, she woke the twins.

'Wake up, sleepy heads,' she told them. As they got out of bed, she ruffled the hair of her son with one hand, and then the hair of her daughter with the other. She gave them each a kiss.

The twins both rubbed the sleep from their eyes before stretching their arms above their heads.

Their mother continued, 'Hurry up or you'll be late! I'll get your breakfast ready while you wash and dress.' Then off she went down the stairs.

Chapter Two

In the dining room, others were stirring too. In the middle of the dining table was a fruit bowl. It was a large fruit bowl that was round and made of wood.

The fruit bowl was the home of the FruitHeads. On this particular morning, there were six FruitHeads sleeping in the bowl.

But wait a minute... maybe there were seven. There were BananaHead and AppleHead. There were OrangeHead and PearHead. GrapeHead and PineappleHead were there as well.

But there was also a newcomer in the fruit bowl today – a big hairy newcomer. He didn't even look like he was a FruitHead!

The first to wake was BananaHead. He yawned loudly, opened his eyes and looked around him. The other FruitHeads were still sleeping.

He could hear PineappleHead snoring, and he could hear GrapeHead talking in his sleep. GrapeHead was saying to himself: 'I must feed the kids, I must feed the kids.' BananaHead smiled and nodded his approval. He knew that GrapeHead took his job very seriously.

OrangeHead was very ladylike and slept peacefully. AppleHead and PearHead were also sleeping, lying happily in each other's arms.

BananaHead felt comfortable. He was with his friends. He yawned and stretched. But as he did so, he was shocked to touch something behind him.

He didn't know what to think. There shouldn't have been anything there! He felt whatever it was with both hands, too scared to turn around and face it.

It was big and hairy – much bigger than any of his friends.

BananaHead called in a loud whisper: 'PineappleHead! PineappleHead! Help! We've got an intruder!'

PineappleHead grunted a couple of times and then turned over to continue sleeping. BananaHead called more loudly.

'PineappleHead! Wake up! Pleeease!'

PineappleHead grunted again, and then opened one eye to look at BananaHead. Soon, both his eyes were wide open, and a yell came from his lips.

'Oh my! What on earth is that?' He was pointing at whatever was behind BananaHead. The other FruitHeads all woke with a start.

'What's going on?' cried OrangeHead.

'What is it?' shouted AppleHead.

'What's up?' said PearHead.

They looked around wildly, and then one by one noticed whoever was standing behind BananaHead.

They all stared, and GrapeHead offered some advice.

'Watch out BananaHead!' he shouted.

That was really helpful... BananaHead already knew that he had to watch out.

He put his hands down slowly, and turned to face whoever was there.

What he saw made his heart miss a beat.

It was a great big, hairy, round thing, brown with a little tuft on top of its head. It was looking straight at him. BananaHead had no idea what it was. Now BananaHead was known to be a brave FruitHead, but even he was scared right at this moment.

'Who are you?' he asked, trembling.

The hairy thing answered in a deep voice: 'I'm CoconutHead.'

'Are you a FruitHead?' BananaHead asked, still a little bit scared.

'I don't know,' came the reply.

The hairy thing looked embarrassed that it didn't know whether it was a FruitHead or not. Its cheeks went a bit red.

'Are you good for little children?' continued BananaHead.

CoconutHead thought about this for a couple of seconds and then replied: 'Yes, I believe I am.'

BananaHead felt a little bit braver now. He looked at CoconutHead, trying to decide whether to believe him or not. He made up his mind.

'Good,' he replied. He was very relieved, and now he was also more confident. 'Do you want to join us today then and help us make sure that the kids eat us?'

CoconutHead looked confused. BananaHead stood up straight and told it like it was.

'CoconutHead, we all have one purpose in life, all of us here.' He looked at the FruitHeads standing around him. 'The kids need good, healthy food, and that's where we FruitHeads come in. We are good for little children. Every day we try and make sure that they eat us rather than PuddingHeads and SweetHeads. We mustn't allow the kids to stuff themselves with unhealthy food, or else they'll become too big and fat, and we don't want that, do we? It's very important that the kids eat us every day!'

'Hear, Hear!' said OrangeHead in her high voice.

'Too right!' cried GrapeHead in his loud voice.

All the FruitHeads agreed. They all knew why they were there.

CoconutHead still didn't really understand though.

'But why do the kids need to eat good food?'

BananaHead told him: 'So that they can grow up to be healthy and strong, so that they can become intelligent and happy. FruitHeads are good food – the kids must eat us!'

All the FruitHeads began to chant: 'Feed the kids! Feed the kids!'

BananaHead waved his hands, prompting them to be quiet. He asked an important question.

'By the way, PearHead, where are the kids?'

'Pardon me?' PearHead replied in his posh voice.

'Where are the kids? It was your turn to watch them and make sure that they take some of us with them for their lunch.'

'Whatever PearHead...' he said, gritting his teeth. 'Anyway, there will be SweetHeads and PuddingHeads out there trying their best to stop us, trying their best to reach the kids first. But we mustn't let them. We mustn't let the kids stuff themselves with bad food. Just remember – the kids need us. FruitHeads rule!'

All the FruitHeads shouted together: 'FruitHeads rule! FruitHeads rule!'

Even CoconutHead joined in: 'FruitHeads rule! FruitHeads rule!'

BananaHead continued.

'Now let's sing the FruitHead song together before we go in search of the kids, shall we?'

All the FruitHeads cheered, and PineappleHead led the singing. He had the best voice.

'We're the FruitHeads, hear us roar,
Fruit for kids! Fruit for kids!
Eat that apple down to its core,
Fruit for kids! Fruit for kids!
Eat a banana to fill your tummy,
Fruit for kids! Fruit for kids!
If you can't find fruit, then ask your Mummy,
Fruit for kids! Fruit for kids!
Eat an orange; it's such a treat,
Fruit for kids! Fruit for kids!
Pears are better than all those sweets,
Fruit for kids! Fruit for kids!
Eat cherries, grapes and melons too,
Fruit for kids! Fruit for kids!
Eat lots of fruit, it's good for you!'

When they'd finished, they all cheered. Then they hugged each other and jumped out of the fruit bowl, one by one. The last to jump was CoconutHead. He really didn't understand what was happening. But he jumped anyway. He felt it was the right thing to do.

Soon the fruit bowl stood empty, and the house was still once more.

Chapter Three

As the FruitHeads jumped from the bowl and landed one at a time, they could feel the wind blowing and found that there was spray in the air.

They had landed on an old galleon – a large, wooden ship – sailing on the High Seas. They could feel the deck rising and falling beneath their feet as the wind caught the ship's huge sails and blew it towards the distant horizon.

'That's right!' shouted PearHead. 'Today the kids have gone to Treasure Chest Island. We have to sail there if we want them to eat us! To your posts FruitHeads!'

'Aye, aye!' they all shouted, and off they went.

BananaHead looked around and saw that each FruitHead was dressed for the part. He himself was at the wheel of the ship and wearing a black hat with gold edging. On his shoulder was a parrot, and one of his legs was wooden. He was the captain of the ship.

'Avast ye shipmates! Load the mainsail!' he shouted.

PearHead and AppleHead were in the rigging. They wore scarves and big earrings. They were very high up. They began to unroll the largest sail just as BananaHead had asked. He wanted as much speed as possible. He knew that the FruitHeads needed to find the twins quickly. These were dangerous waters.

'What do you see, lookout?' yelled BananaHead, cupping his hand to his mouth to make it easier for PineappleHead to hear him.

PineappleHead was in the crow's nest at the top of the mast. He had a telescope and was looking all around.

'N o t h i n g, Captain!' he answered.

'Keep looking. We mustn't drop our guard! And you two...' he pointed at GrapeHead and O r a n g e H e a d, '...scrub those decks!'

GrapeHead and OrangeHead didn't argue. They put their backs into it and made sure that their ship had the cleanest deck any ship had ever had.

BananaHead puffed out his chest and smiled. He ran a tight ship. Just then, he felt a tap on his shoulder. BananaHead jumped and turned around. It was CoconutHead. In all the excitement, he'd forgotten about him.

'What can I do, Captain?'

BananaHead thought about it.

'I'll tell you what, you can raise the FruitHead flag!'

And that's exactly what CoconutHead did – he raised the FruitHead flag.

He could see the scowling faces of JellyHead, TreacleHead and IceCreamHead – three of the most fearsome PuddingHeads!

But worse than that, BananaHead could see that there were SweetHeads on board, too. The SweetHeads were really bad news, and there were hordes of them. There were JellyBeanHeads, MintHeads, ToffeeHeads and even a couple of LollyHeads. They were shouting and screaming, and waving cutlasses in the air. This was not good. If the PuddingHeads' ship caught up with them, the FruitHeads would be lost!

But it was no use – they couldn't escape.

The PuddingHeads' ship slowly gained on them and pulled alongside. As it did so, BananaHead heard JellyHead shout: 'SweetHeads! Prepare to board!'

All the SweetHeads grabbed hold of ropes and swung across to the FruitHeads' ship, shouting and yelling, whooping and screaming.

They were singing too:

'Oh, although we're only small,
We are having such a ball,
As we chase the FruitHeads' ship across the seas!

'Cos we're really tough, all right,
And we really like a fight,
As we swing across, we shout: "We'll win with ease!"'

A couple of MintHeads fell into the sea as they crossed to the FruitHeads' ship, but enough of them made it so that fighting was pointless. The FruitHeads were badly outnumbered and they knew it. They could do nothing but surrender. The SweetHeads continued to sing:

'As we land upon the deck,
All the FruitHeads cry: "Oh Heck!"
As they realise they're well and truly beaten!

For we have won the day,
They can't even run away,
And for once the scummy FruitHeads won't get eaten!'

The SweetHeads were now roaring and shouting even louder, and still waving their cutlasses in the air – and they were still singing!

'Oh, we SweetHeads have had fun,
We are proud of what we've done,
So to all of you, please take this as a warning!

We SweetHeads are the best,
We are better than the rest,
And the twins will eat us up this very morning!'

The FruitHeads stood on the deck, surrounded by SweetHeads. They had their hands in the air and were looking very sorry for themselves. A gangplank was placed between the two ships, and the FruitHeads were forced to cross to the PuddingHeads' ship.

As they stepped on board, the PuddingHeads were there to greet them. BananaHead saw that each of the PuddingHeads was dressed as a pirate and JellyHead was missing one hand. In its place was a hook.

'So, BananaHead, we meet again,' he said. 'And this time it looks like we have the upper hand... ha, ha, ha!'

He waved his hook in the air. He was laughing. It was a horrible laugh.

The other PuddingHeads joined in, and so did the SweetHeads. BananaHead didn't like this at all.

'What are you going to do with us?' he asked.

'I'm not sure,' said JellyHead, 'but it won't be pleasant, you can be certain of that! And you can forget all about being eaten by the kids today! It's our turn!'

A big cheer went up from the PuddingHeads and the SweetHeads.

From the FruitHeads, all you could hear was a quiet groan.

'Throw them in the hold!' commanded JellyHead.

IceCreamHead walked over to a big iron-barred hatch, which covered a square hole in the middle of the deck and lifted it up.

It was heavy and made a loud creaking noise as it opened. Inside the hold below it looked very cold and dark. It really wasn't going to be pleasant for the FruitHeads.

The SweetHeads pushed the FruitHeads in, one by one, cheering as each one dropped into the hold. The last to go was CoconutHead. JellyHead stopped him with his hook before he could follow the others.

'CoconutHead, there's a big surprise waiting for you down there…' he said. With that he pushed CoconutHead towards the hole, kicking him from behind as he did so.

CoconutHead fell in with a thud, and IceCreamHead slammed the hatch behind him, turning the key in a big padlock as he did so to make sure that the FruitHeads couldn't escape.

Chapter Five

It was certainly dark in the hold, but not so dark that they couldn't see anything.

'Is everyone all right?' asked BananaHead.

'I'm fine,' replied AppleHead.

'Of course!' said GrapeHead.

'Yes indeed!' cried PearHead.

'I think so,' whispered OrangeHead.

'As well as can be expected,' sighed PineappleHead.

They were a courageous bunch – well most of them anyway...

'I'm not sure actually...' murmured CoconutHead.

There was a moment's silence, and then from behind BananaHead came another voice.

'I'm not sure either...'

BananaHead whirled around.

'Who's there?!'

Another large, dark, hairy figure emerged from the deepest shadows of the hold. All of the FruitHeads took a step back, not sure whether the figure was friend or foe – all except one.

CoconutHead ran forward and threw his arms around the stranger.

'Dad!' he sobbed. 'I thought I'd lost you forever!'

'Son! Is it really you?'

They hugged each other, not sure whether to laugh or cry.

'Son, you make an old timer really happy. I just wish that it wasn't under these circumstances.'

They hugged each other again.

'Dad, meet my friends. These are the FruitHeads.'

CoconutHead introduced them all, one by one, and then asked his father a question.

'Dad, where have you been?'

'Ah, that's a long story, son.'

'Well, we haven't got anything better to do, have we? Tell me!'

'I suppose not. Make yourselves comfortable then, and I'll begin.'

They all sat down on the floor of the hold and listened to CoconutHead's father as he told his story.

Chapter Six

'I was born at the top of the highest palm tree on Treasure Chest Island, as was his mother.'

He put his arm around his son's shoulders.

'We were happy there together, especially when this one came along.'

He looked proudly at his son.

'We were a family, a happy family. Then one day there was a big storm. It came from the East. We could see it coming and braced ourselves for it, but there was nothing we could do. It was too strong. It made the sea wild, and blew the palm trees until they bent down almost to the beach.

'One by one, we were blown from our home. Your mother went first. I never saw her again.' He wiped a tear from his eye, and paused for a while.

'I held on as long as I could, but then I was taken, too, leaving you behind, son. That was my greatest regret. I never wanted to leave you behind, but the wind grabbed me and threw me into the sea...'

He paused once more, just looking at his son for a while. Then he continued.

'CoconutHeads are good swimmers, so I was fine, but I bobbed around in the sea for days. I really thought that I would never find land again.

'Then one day I felt a nudge from below, so I ducked under the water and came face to face with a huge FishHead. Luckily for me, she was a friendly FishHead and wished me no harm.

'Are you all right?' she asked me. I told her that I really wanted to find land again, that I wanted to do my job and be eaten by the kids.

'She said, 'No problem! I can help you there!' and pushed me all the way back to land. She was lovely.

'I was really hopeful then. I thought that I would be eaten at long last, but I was so unlucky. No sooner had I landed then the PuddingHeads arrived and took me prisoner. I really don't know why. I've been here in this hold ever since. I'm so old now that I'm not sure that the kids would even want to eat me anymore...'

More tears rolled down his face. His son gave him a hug.

'Don't worry, Dad. Everything will be OK now.'

His father looked at him.

'You're wrong son. You're all in the same position as me now. There's no escape from here. None of us will ever be eaten by the kids...'

A silence fell over all of them. The FruitHeads said nothing. They just looked at each other with shock on their faces. The thought of never being eaten by the little boy and the little girl horrified them!

At that point, they heard the PuddingHeads start to sing. The PuddingHeads were on deck and obviously celebrating:

'We're PuddingHeads and we are sweet,
For any kid we're such a treat,
We taste so good, we're so much fun,
There's plenty here for everyone!
Pour cream on us, or chocolate sauce,
Or even maple syrup of course!
Then eat us 'til you've had your fill,
Then eat some more until you're ill!'

As they finished the song, they cheered.

The FruitHeads looked up, all thinking the same thing – how could they escape?

No one had an answer.

A few minutes passed, and then it was too late anyway. The big iron-barred hatch opened above them, and JellyHead peered in.

'Right, you lot, up here now – and that includes you two hairy boys.'

'Hairy boys? We're not hairy boys! We're FruitHeads!' said CoconutHead with a touch of pride. At least he thought he knew what he was now.

All of them slowly climbed the steps and came out into the daylight. They stood on the deck, shielding their eyes from the sun. It was painful after the darkness of the hold.

BananaHead stepped on to the deck, and once he could see properly again, he looked out to sea – his own

ship was nowhere to be seen. It must have drifted away while they were being held prisoner. How would they ever get to the twins now?

The FruitHeads found themselves faced by the three PuddingHeads. All around were SweetHeads – sitting on barrels and standing on the deck.

JellyHead spoke up.

'OK, FruitHeads, which one of you is in charge?'

The FruitHeads all looked at each other, and BananaHead stepped forward.

'I am,' he said.

'Can you swim?' asked JellyHead.

BananaHead hesitated before he replied: '...I don't know. I've never tried.'

'Oh good,' said JellyHead. 'I'm going to enjoy this!'

JellyHead wasn't very nice.

He pointed to a plank of wood that stuck out from the side of the ship.

'If you would be so kind, BananaHead...'

BananaHead knew what was happening. He'd heard about this. He was going to have to walk the plank!

He would have to walk to the end of the plank and jump into the sea below, where he'd either sink or float away into the distance, never to be seen again. It wasn't much of a choice.

He moved bravely towards the plank, trying not to show the other FruitHeads how scared he was. The SweetHeads were cheering and JellyHead prodded him in the back with his hook, encouraging him to walk faster.

When he reached the plank, he stepped on to it and turned around.

'JellyHead, you're making a mistake,' he said.

'And what mistake is that?'

'We know where the kids are, and you don't.'

'How do you know that we don't?'

'Because you're sailing in the wrong direction!'

'Don't be stupid, BananaHead. You're just trying to trick me!'

'You really think so?' BananaHead answered. And before JellyHead could reply, BananaHead ran along the plank and jumped into the sea below.

As he jumped, he shouted 'FruitHeads rule!' and then all anyone heard was a loud splash and nothing more.

The FruitHeads looked at each other in horror.

The SweetHeads cheered, and the PuddingHeads laughed – all except JellyHead.

He looked uncertain. BananaHead had been right. JellyHead really didn't know if he was going in the right direction or not. He had no idea where the twins were today.

He shouted 'Quiet!' to his crew.

Everyone became silent.

He turned to the remaining FruitHeads, including the two CoconutHeads. They all looked very scared.

'Right, you lot! Tell me where the kids are, or you'll all be set adrift in a small boat!'

He was threatening them and they were frightened – but they were also brave. GrapeHead spoke up for all of them.

'We don't know where the kids are! Only BananaHead knew. He was our leader. So do your worst, JellyHead!'

JellyHead looked at GrapeHead closely and then roared in frustration.

'Put them in a boat and lower them over the side!' he shouted.

The JellyBeanHeads pushed the remaining FruitHeads and the two CoconutHeads into a boat. It was only a small boat, so it was a very tight squeeze. But there was no mercy. They were lowered over the side and set adrift.

As soon as they had drifted a short distance away from the ship, they could hear JellyHead shouting:

'Set sail you lazy So and Sos! We need to find the kids!'

They saw the sails go up and the PuddingHeads' ship began to gather speed, moving further and further away until it was just a small dot in the distance.

As BananaHead had noticed, the FruitHeads' own ship had long since drifted out of sight.

Chapter Seven

OrangeHead was in tears, and none of the others was particularly happy.

GrapeHead spoke first.

'Well, thank you, PearHead!'

'What do you mean?'

'If it wasn't for you, we would have fed the kids before they left this morning, and we wouldn't be stuck here in the middle of the ocean!'

'And we wouldn't have lost BananaHead...' whimpered OrangeHead.

'How dare you! I told you that it wasn't my turn to keep an eye on the kids, it was AppleHead's turn!' said PearHead.

'Oh, that's right, blame it on me!' replied AppleHead.

CoconutHead and his father said nothing. They just sat there glumly.

Just then, a voice piped up.
   'Now, now, FruitHeads, please calm
down – did you miss me?'
   BananaHead appeared over the
side of the boat. It was a miracle!

'BananaHead!' they all shouted together.

'We thought we'd lost you!' cried OrangeHead.

'I'm so glad to see you!' gushed AppleHead.

'How marvellous!' said PearHead.

'How lucky can you get!' exclaimed GrapeHead.

'So you can swim!' acknowledged PineappleHead.

'Actually, no I can't,' replied BananaHead, climbing over the side of the boat.

'So how come you're here?'

'I had some help from your old friend,' he said, smiling at CoconutHead's father. 'Look.'

The FruitHeads looked over the side of the boat and what did they see? It was FishHead! FishHead had saved BananaHead.

It brought a tear to the eye of CoconutHead's father. He was so pleased to see his old friend once again.

'FishHead! How are you?' he asked.

'Fine, thank you. And so pleased to see that you're still around! How have you been keeping?'

'Not well, I'm afraid. I've been held prisoner by the PuddingHeads all this time, so I still haven't been able to feed the kids yet.'

'That's too bad. Maybe I can help again?'

BananaHead spoke up.

'Could you? We really need to get to Treasure Chest Island before the PuddingHeads get there. We know that the kids are there.'

'Of course I can help. We FishHeads want to feed the kids ourselves, and we're quite happy to help you FruitHeads along the way!'

'There's only one problem,' said BananaHead, 'the PuddingHeads are way ahead of us.'

'I thought they were going in the wrong direction,' said OrangeHead.

'Unfortunately not,' said BananaHead, 'I lied.'

They all looked at him as though he was mad. FruitHeads were GoodHeads. They never lied!

'Sorry, I thought it was for a good cause,' apologised BananaHead. He was very embarrassed, but nobody seemed to mind too much. Especially not GrapeHead:

'I didn't tell JellyHead the truth either,' he said, sheepishly. 'PearHead knew where the kids were, since he was the one who went to look for them this morning. But I couldn't tell JellyHead that!'

All the FruitHeads agreed that BananaHead and GrapeHead had been right to bend the truth on this occasion.

FishHead interrupted.
  'Anyway, don't worry about the PuddingHeads. We can easily outpace them. Tie that rope to the front of the boat, BananaHead, and throw the other end into the water.'

BananaHead did as he was told, and after a few seconds, the FruitHeads felt the boat move forward. It went faster and faster, and they soon had sight of the PuddingHeads' ship once more.

PearHead was at the front of the boat, and looked into the water to see what was pulling them. He was amazed by what he saw. There wasn't just one FishHead pulling them, there were hundreds – they were all different shapes and sizes, all pulling as hard as they could.

As the boat reached the island, the FishHeads dropped the rope and let the boat glide to a gentle stop on the beach.

The FruitHeads and the two CoconutHeads jumped out and turned to wave goodbye to their new friends. They were surprised to see a couple of FishHeads coming out of the water, running towards them. The FishHeads wanted to be eaten by the twins as well. They were also good for the kids.

'I didn't know that you could run,' said PineappleHead, laughing. 'Thanks for your help by the way.'

'Not at all,' said FishHead. 'Now let's get to the kids before the PuddingHeads and SweetHeads get here!'

They turned and started to run up the beach towards the mouths of the little boy and the little girl.

'Just a minute!' shouted the two CoconutHeads.

Everyone stopped and turned to listen to what they had to say.

The father spoke.

'Everyone – I'd like to thank you so much for bringing me here. This is all I've ever dreamed about. I don't know how I can ever repay you.'

He was crying tears of joy.

BananaHead walked over to him and put a hand on his shoulder.

'You don't have to. Just being here, and letting the kids eat you is enough. Once we've all been eaten, they'll be much too full to eat SweetHeads and PuddingHeads today!'

'FruitHeads rule!' shouted all the FruitHeads.

'And FishHeads, too – don't forget the FishHeads!' shouted the FishHeads.

'And the VegHeads!'

They all turned to see CarrotHead and BroccoliHead running along the beach to join them.

'Good to see you, VegHeads!' said BananaHead, 'I was beginning to wonder where you'd got to today!'

'Better late than never!' said CarrotHead.

And with that, they all ran up the beach and into the gaping mouths of the twins.

Chapter Eight

The last in was BananaHead. The others had all been eaten already. He turned to look out to sea. He was smiling. The PuddingHead ship was still a long way off, and the twins were just about full. Before he went however, he decided to sing one more song:

'This is me, BananaHead,
Where I want to be,
Standing near a child's mouth,
Looking out to sea.
My friends have all been eaten,
And now it is my turn,
This is what I've longed for,
As I hope you've learned.
There I see the BadHeads,
Sailing on the sea,
All of them are scowling,
And shouting angrily!
I'll watch them for a while,
And then run into the tummy,
Of the little child whose mouth I'm near,
The child who thinks I'm yummy!
And even though I've gone today,
There is no need for sorrow,
For you will find us FruitHeads
Sitting in the bowl tomorrow!'

Coming Shortly!

The FruitHeads
and the
Running Race

The FruitHeads
in the
Wild West

Contact Details

Websites:
www.jesspress.co.uk/www.thefruitheads.co.uk

Address:
JessPress Ltd
'The FruitHeads'
PO Box 404,
Tunbridge Wells,
Kent. TN3 0WZ
0870 7662648

Email:
info@thefruitheads.co.uk

Please see website for details of supported charities.
JessPress pledges to support charities that
"Promote the health and happiness of children both in the
UK and around the World"